Dear Parent:

Your child's love of reading starts here!

Every child learns to read in a different way and at his or her own speed. Some go back and forth between reading levels and read favorite books again and again. Others read through each level in order. You can help your young reader improve and become more confident by encouraging his or her own interests and abilities. From books your child reads with you to the first books he or she reads alone, there are I Can Read Books for every stage of reading:

SHARED READING
Basic language, word repetition, and whimsical illustrations, ideal for sharing with your emergent reader

BEGINNING READING
Short sentences, familiar words, and simple concepts for children eager to read on their own

READING WITH HELP
Engaging stories, longer sentences, and language play for developing readers

READING ALONE
Complex plots, challenging vocabulary, and high-interest topics for the independent reader

I Can Read Books have introduced children to the joy of reading since 1957. Featuring award-winning authors and illustrators and a fabulous cast of beloved characters, I Can Read Books set the standard for beginning readers.

A lifetime of discovery begins with the magical words **"I Can Read!"**

Visit www.icanread.com for information on enriching your child's reading experience.

Be safe! Always cook with an adult. Don't touch
sharp knives or hot stoves and ovens! And always
wash your hands before and after cooking.

To Nana, Mom, and Dayo!
—O.R.-P.

For my loving parents
—L.M.

I Can Read® and I Can Read Book® are trademarks of HarperCollins Publishers.
Balzer + Bray is an imprint of HarperCollins Publishers.

Makeda Makes a Birthday Treat
Text copyright © 2023 by Olugbemisola Rhuday-Perkovich
Illustrations copyright © 2023 by Lydia Mba
All rights reserved. Printed in the United States of America.
No part of this book may be used or reproduced in any manner whatsoever without written permission except
in the case of brief quotations embodied in critical articles and reviews. For information address HarperCollins
Children's Books, a division of HarperCollins Publishers, 195 Broadway, New York, NY 10007.
www.icanread.com

Library of Congress Control Number: 2022045114
ISBN 978-0-06-321724-9 (pbk) — ISBN 978-0-06-321726-3 (trade bdg)

The artist used Adobe Photoshop and Procreate to create the digital illustrations for this book.
Typography by Caitlin E. D. Stamper
23 24 25 26 27 LB 10 9 8 7 6 5 4 3 2 1
First Edition

Makeda Makes
a Birthday Treat

By Olugbemisola Rhuday-Perkovich
Pictures by Lydia Mba

BALZER + BRAY

An Imprint of HarperCollins*Publishers*

Makeda loved to make marvelous things.

Like robot puppets

and cardboard cities,

funny faces for baby cousins,

magic potions, and felt flower crowns.

Makeda made pretty presents
that made Nana smile
and magnificent messes
that made Momma frown.

"You're on my side of the room,"
said her sister, Candace.
Candace loved to make rules.

The next day was Makeda's birthday!
At school, birthdays meant that
the class sang special birthday songs!
Ms. Evelyn read a birthday book!
And the birthday kid
brought cupcakes to share.

Makeda did not want to bring cupcakes.

She wanted to bring

marvelous coconut drops.

"Nobody brings coconut drops,"
said Candace.

"Everybody brings cupcakes,"
said her brother, James.

"Makeda is not nobody," said Momma.

"And she is not everybody."

10

"I want to share things I love,"

said Makeda.

"Coconut drops and back home stories!"

That night, Makeda made sweet, spicy coconut drops with Momma and Nana.

They sang while they cooked.

They danced and dropped the drops.

Nana made a special pot of tea.

She told back home stories

of mango trees and clear island waters.

Next, Makeda and Daddy made a box

for her birthday coconut drops.

She wrote *marvelous*

in fancy letters across the top.

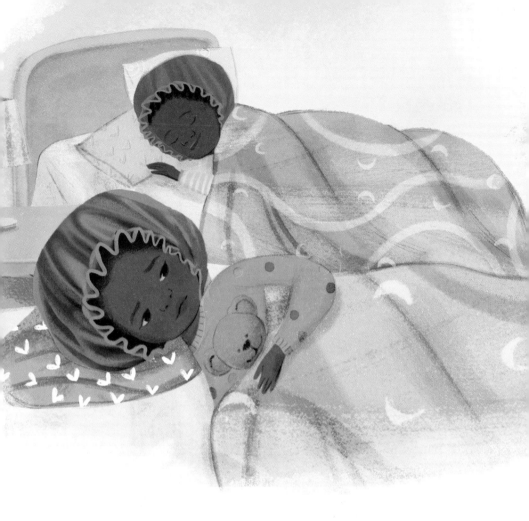

Later in bed, she lay awake.

Robert was always first to stand up

for birthday cupcakes.

What if he didn't stand up

for coconut drops?

The next morning at school,

Makeda held her marvelous box high.

"Birthday cupcakes!"

said her best friend, Glory.

"I like chocolate and lemon."

"I like cupcakes too," said Makeda.

"But today I brought coconut drops."

"Will you share cupcakes after the coconut drops?" Glory asked.

"I will share my family's story," said Makeda.

"Coconut drops are a special treat in many countries."

"Cupcakes are a special treat in Ms. Evelyn's class," said Glory.

Makeda frowned and put down her box.
What if her classmates did not care
about sunshine songs
and back home stories?

After math games,

it was finally time for

Makeda's Marvelous

Birthday Celebration!

Her classmates sang.

Ms. Evelyn sang the loudest.

And the most off-key.

Makeda took a deep breath.

Glory squeezed her hand.

Then Makeda stood and opened

the beautiful box she had made.

Her classmates leaned in to look.

"Those cupcakes look funny," said Robert.

Denise made a rude face.

"Did you make a mistake?" asked Lu.

"I made my special treat,"

said Makeda. "These are

my Marvelous Coconut Drops."

Everyone looked at Makeda.

Everyone looked at the box.

Everyone looked back at Makeda.

Ticktock went the classroom clock.

"Who would like to try coconut drops?"
asked Ms. Evelyn.

"I'm getting cupcakes after school,"
said Denise.

"No you're not," said Mark.

Then Glory stood up.

"I would like one," she said.

Glory bit. She chewed.

She swallowed. She smiled.

"It tastes like a sweet sunny day!"

She took another bite.

"I love birthday coconut drops!"

"I make them with Nana and my momma,"
said Makeda.

"We drop the drops, we dance, we sing.
And Nana tells back home stories."

Robert stood up.

"My daddy makes stollen

for a sweet treat," he said.

"I would like to try a coconut drop."

He bit. He smiled.

"I can taste the stories!"

Soon many of Makeda's classmates
lined up for coconut drops.
They told stories about
their own family treats.

"I love halo-halo," said Ms. Evelyn.
"It is made from shaved ice, milk,
and sometimes sweet beans."

"My favorite treat also has beans,"
said Glory. "But it is not sweet.
It is called moi moi.
I eat it for breakfast."

"Beans are not a treat," said Taylor.

"Treats can be different

for different people," said Makeda.

"I love mangú," said Yahaira.
"It is not sweet. It is a little sour.
On Sundays, my abuelo makes it
with plantains,
and we read the newspaper."
"Your abuelo reads the paper,"
said Lu. "*You* can't."
She liked to give reminders
and get gold stars.

"Our stories make our treats special,"

said Ms. Evelyn.

"Thank you, Makeda,

for sharing your joy!"

Some classmates had seconds.

Some ate their own snacks.

All shared more songs and stories.

After school, Makeda and Glory
made more coconut drops.
They also made cupcakes
and a big, colorful salad.
"Friendship treats are always sweet,"
said Makeda.
"And that is MARVELOUS!"